Create Destruction

Create Destruction

A NOVEL IN VERSE BY

RYAN A. KOVACS

PHiR Publishing
San Antonio

Copyright © 2023 by Ryan A. Kovacs

All rights reserved. No part of this book may be reproduced without permission. If you would like to use material from the book (other than for review purposes), please contact permissions@phirpublishing.com.

PHiR Publishing
San Antonio, TX
phirpublishing.com

First edition: March 2023

ISBN: 9798986745220
Library of Congress Control Number: 2022919857

Printed in the United States of America

This book is dedicated to my children, Everly and Jameson, as a reminder to them that we all have a choice in life.

"The intention that man should be happy is not in the plan of Creation."
-Sigmund Freud

CREATE

Sequence I
Control

Ryan A. Kovacs

Create Destruction

"Do you know what man's greatest creation is?
Hmm?"
He asked the silent audience.

"Most would argue that life
is man's greatest creation.
Your doctors
religious folk
mothers
biologists
and even children, I dare say
would all argue
that life
is man's greatest creation.

But do you know what it takes to create life?

        Just a man and a woman fucking.
              That's all.

There doesn't need to be a connection—
no passion or
love or
even an interest in the other person
in order to create a human life.
I know it sounds crass
but the X and Y are not the means to a beginning
yet the means to an end.
You see, without life
we could not have the power to create
which is why the power to destroy, is so much greater.

Creation
is not a choice—
                it is a consequence.

Destruction
on the other hand
is the undeniable action
that man chooses—
          the very thing he creates.

And that is what we are here today to prove.
Many of you are skeptics, I know
and I understand why.
To harness this kind of power
we have only dipped our fingers in to
is hard to fathom.
But I assure you
we are ahead of the world
in this race for dominance
and absolute power.

                Behold!"

He paused for a moment
allowing the red curtains to be pulled back
exposing me to eyes
that would judge and damn me.

              "The first human bomb!"

The crowd's elation was halted
with brief disappointment
as they gazed at me
standing behind three-inch glass
and wall-to-ceiling
smooth-pressed concrete
with my half-naked body
covered only in my pee-stained underwear—
      the true sign of his accomplishment
            and mine of submission and embarrassment.

I stared at the preponderance
with hollow eyes that only yearned

Create Destruction

for comfort.
And yet, my uncomforted ability
to give them what they desired
was soon at hand while Dr. Larson's voice
reverberated through the intercom system in my enclosure.
"What I am here to demonstrate today
is but a small glimpse
of the power we have begun to harness.
For safety precautions
I encourage everyone to place
the lead vests and glasses on in front of you before we begin."

Dr. Larson did as he had instructed the others
before speaking once more.
"Imagine for a moment
a weapon you cannot see coming."
The lights dimmed
until all I could see was my pathetic
skin and bone reflection in the glass before me
while the people in the crowd were drowned out by obscurity.
"Imagine a weapon that upon firing
needs no reloading or cool down
yet detonates no differently than a grenade.
It can self-heal
feels no pain
and follows every order it is given
never failing or having fault."

His words echoed in my mind
like a train derailing off a mountainside.
I was programmed to respond
to his triggers
through a rigorous thought-terminating process
that proved to be sufficient
to control the United States' greatest asset—
                                                           me.

He was the gunman
and I was the gun.
In so, wherever he would point
I would shoot.

Ryan A. Kovacs

There was a point in my life when I had a choice
and my last choice was to give up
my free will.

My father sat before me
with his sleeve rolled up.
His right arm but a ghost of a reminder
of what used to be there.
It was the first of many things taken from him.

The Korean War
was still a wound to his past—
a scab that could be picked
or scratched at
just to feel something real.
Yet, he was strong for me
seeing my potential
and placing in my mind
the confidence I would need going forward.

"Son,"
he stated softly
"This is a great responsibility to undertake…"

I cut him off
"But I could save so many."

"At what cost though?"
he begged.

I looked at him sharply
and extended my right hand
in exchange for his
which could not be met.

"A far less cost than you or mom have paid."

A tear appeared in his eye
while he grabbed my hand with

the only hand he had left
"If this is your choice
then I will not stop you."

Rising from his chair he turned around
approaching Dr. Larson in his long white coat
who held a clipboard with legal documents
that my father whisked a pen on
signing and dating
surrendering his parental authority
to the man who would turn me into
the deadliest weapon known to humanity.

Dr. Larson spoke at me
"Thomas, would you please demonstrate
for our respective audience
a small flare."

His demand was masked as a request
as I knew the consequences had I resisted.
The intercom rehearsed the first words:

"Head...

Boulevard...

Six."

I rose from the metal chair
taking a deep breath
remembering to concentrate and focus my energy.
Opening my palm
I extended my fingers as wide as they could go
and began to flex every tendon and muscle fiber within them
until the pressure began to build in my forearm.

Within seconds my hand began to glow neon
while steam polluted the cool air around me.
Harnessing such vigor was no different than having a fever
as chills ran up and down my spine
and sweat oozed out my pores.

Dr. Larson's face was pleased
"Now, touch the chair, Thomas."

I turned around to grip the top of the chair
but before my fingers had touched the steel
it began to bow and sag with the presence of heat
being emitted from my hand.
In a moments time
the chair had absorbed my intensity
as it melted to the floor
appearing as a pile of muck.

Create Destruction

With my light I could see the audience as they sat in awe
while Dr. Larson smirked in achievement
"Magnificent, is it not?"

A few hands from the crowd flew into the air
"We have two more demonstrations before questions
thank you,"
Dr. Larson stated eagerly.

"Thomas, if you would please face the door now,"
he demanded.
With it, a wave of guards entered the room
storming it like a raid
with batons in hand.
"Begin,"
Dr. Larson spoke into the microphone
as the men attacked me from every angle
bashing my face and body
opening gaping wounds
while flesh tore and bones broke
retiring me to the floor on my hands and knees.
The guards halted
and the intercom rehearsed once more:

"Park...

Right...

Flower."

Within seconds my lesions closed
and blood stopped leaking
while my bones reattached internally
giving me strength to stand again.
Barely out of breath
I closed my eyes
making peace with what would follow.

"Breathtaking, is it not?"
Dr. Larson asked rhetorically.
Readying himself for the final demonstration
he spoke once more
"Thomas, proceed to the back of the bunker now
for the final demonstration."

The blast doors behind me peeled open
like an onion
giving off the aroma of cow feces.
At a distance
two cows stood chained to the concrete ground
eating a few strings of grass before them
with their tails swaying along their backside.
As I approached them
not an ounce of remorse filled my heart or mind
for the creatures who would soon suffer at my hands
while I did an about-face
watching the blast doors close like eyelids
presenting me with nothing but obscurity.
The loud siren rang below the yellow flashing light
indicating the test was clear for demonstration.
The intercom vocalized loudly:

"Worn...

Ciao..."

Create Destruction

My body froze.
Trapped within a mindset which was no longer mine.
I tensed
unable to break free of the hold
that invisibly kept me grounded
to the words that gave me power
yet left me powerless to control.
With brief hesitation
I inhaled deeply
while my reality shrunk around me
until my only focus
was on the next word that would follow…

"Destroy."

Ryan A. Kovacs

I awoke to the smell of freshly cleaned sheets
that tickled my nostrils
as if a feather danced inside
caressing each nose hair that sent my olfactory recall
to a time before that room.
I was no longer in my pee-stained underwear
but rather comfortable
with the formed sheet laid atop my body.
I sighed at the thought of my accomplishment
recognizing the torment that was my immediate past
I no longer was enduring.

The door opened
and Dr. Larson entered contentedly
with his hands folded
"You have no clue what you have done my boy."
I sat up in suspense
afraid of my potential failure and his expectations.

"You have altered the course of history,"
he stated with great jubilation.
"All our arduous work
and suffering of humankind
will now bow to our imminent power.
The United States of America will never be preyed upon
again because of you."

"Did I do well?"
I asked with naivety.

"Oh, you did exceptionally well."
He smiled his evil grin
and his tell was obvious.
Dr. Larson may have been good at keeping secrets
never exposing himself or his intentions
but the one thing he could never control
was his body language.

Create Destruction

My mother always told me that
we say more with our bodies than with our mouths
and nothing could be truer about the mad doctor
and I suppose
nothing could be truer about me ...

Ryan A. Kovacs

It was my 10th birthday when my mother passed away.
Her body riddled with cancer
and her insides about as toxic as hydrogen sulfide
they feared burying her in a cemetery
that she might pollute the earth
and pose a threat to my existence.
Against her wishes and my fathers'
they cremated her
almost completely erasing her existence from this world.

Create Destruction

The only thing different about that birthday
was the fact that my mother died
otherwise it was the same thing I had been used to
seeing her slowly deteriorate
as if she were a rock and the cancer was a slow drip of water
eventually eroding her down until she no longer had form.

Prior to my birth
my mother had been diagnosed with pancreatic cancer.
The doctors told her that she had to choose between
receiving radiation therapy
or going through the pregnancy untreated
risking the cancer spreading.
Her response was very typical when she told them
"Why would you think the same chemicals
that likely gave me cancer in the first place
would save me in the end?
I'll take my chances without them
and hope the child cures me."

Those were words my mother possibly regretted
at some point in her life
when she signed a waiver to be treated by the government
that claimed to have her best interests in mind
putting their hands in the womb
of their greatest plan yet.
In turn, my mother was a byproduct
of the greatest thing man had created—
the Atomic Bomb.

She and my father were the vision
of what the bomb could accomplish
but what they had dreamt
would become the nightmare that was born
paving the long and darkened path
that ultimately led to me.

At the time it did not seem likely.
The puppeteers
coordinated
compiled
and contradicted
their own theories of rhetoric and non-sequential data
stirred a pot of
this
that
and the other thing
which ultimately
created the formula for destruction.

Create Destruction

The Manhattan Project was more than just
the greatest compilation of human minds and virtues
led by a man whose only belief was to provide a result.
Once the project was completed though
there simply was no more use for them
and thus, they were discarded.

That was until Dr. Larson posed the idea
that the link between the greatest minds in the world
were about to become the largest lab rats
the country would never know about.

Shortly after test phases for the Atomic Bomb started
Dr. Larson had all the dormitory rooms bugged
checking in on who was most sexually active
alongside promoting sexual activity
amongst the doctors and scientists
knowing that their human needs would need to be satisfied
with only present company.
With the wide ratio of emotion and thought processes
paired with long work hours and food rations
the perfect storm brewed among the men and women
who starved for affection and relief from the stresses of each day.
My mother's friend Ginny was the first to get pregnant
and before her second trimester
she was removed from the program
never to be heard from again.
Everyone speculated of course
thinking she was transported away to have her baby safely
however, conveniently that was the first absence Dr. Larson took.

Ryan A. Kovacs

He was a man of intricate and maniacal thought processes
under the ruse of an intrigued and idealistic scientist.
His archaic and barbaric fundamental study techniques
were never exploited until he met me
which renders the thought
was he always that way
or did I bring it out in him?

Create Destruction

"I want to show you some pictures Thomas
and when you look at them
study them for a moment.
Really concentrate on the image you see
before you tell me the word it describes."

I nodded coherently
sitting uneasy in the metal chair
having the only thought crossing my mind
are there no other comfortable chairs like his?

Placing a flash card in front of me
was a portrait of myself—
the picture they took of me
when I first got to the underground facility.

Staring at it, I could not help but notice my greatest physical
insecurity—
my widow's peak.
Due to my unusually oval shaped skull
my hair seemed to grow inward
pushing all the hairs towards the center
giving me what I always believed to be an ugly point
that served no purpose.
Conveniently it also made me stick out
amongst the other children I had gone to grade school with.

Some of them made fun of me for it
and once given the choice
I shaved all my hair off
only to be more disappointed that the darkness of my hair
matched with my milky white skin
left the outline of my hairline like a tattoo
magnifying my Eddie Munster look.

With pure disgust I answered Dr. Larson
"Head."

At what cost do we allow the subconscious to control us?
It is there that we instinctually act or react
never allowing thoughts to hinder consequences
yet it begs the question—
is it already preordained?

Dr. Larson looked on at me
"Now, Thomas
I am going to show you another picture
and this time I want you to answer immediately.
Do you understand?"

I nodded in compliance.
Raising from the table
was the exact same picture he'd shown me
and to my confusion I responded
"Face."

He grinned with displeasure
placing the card down on the table
while waving a guard towards me.
I did not understand.
I had done what he instructed
and within my confusion
felt a sharp pinch in my neck
followed abruptly with the tightening of straps
across my wrists and ankles.

Bound to the chair
I looked at Dr. Larson
pleading with my eyes while he followed up
"I am going to show you a picture again.
I cannot emphasize enough
the importance of you responding on impulse.
Do not think!
Rather, feel the word exit your mouth."
Once more he revealed the same picture of me
as I replied
"Head."

Create Destruction

Instead of a pinch in my neck however
I felt the tingling numbness in my fingers and toes
realizing how tight the restraints were
I slowly began to panic.
Dr. Larson spoke once more
"Again, tell me what you see now."

Placing the picture before me
he slammed his hand on the table
"Again!"

"Head."

Flipping up another card
"Again damnit!"

"But I can't feel my fingers and toes!"
I exclaimed in discomfort.

"Stop thinking about what you can't do.
Feel the word
and say it again."

"Head."

"Louder!"
He exclaimed.

"Head!"

"Louder! Again!"

"Head!"

Then he repeated loudly after me

"Head."

Then suddenly
my wrist restraints loosened
falling to the ground with a gentle tap
as I rose from the chair
unable to feel my hands slamming on the table
as they pulsated a gentle glow
before blood rushed to my extremities
allowing me to feel the cool metal table underneath my fingertips.

"Good,"
Dr. Larson declared.
"You are ready to begin."

Create Destruction

What was superficially a test of my subconscious
was in conjunction unknown to me
just how powerful that one word would become
in the months that followed
as I became the ultimate specimen
of both torture and psychological warfare
surrounded by a man whose curiosity far outweighed his fears.

Dr. Larson maintained his composure
during most of my successful and failed attempts
at being what he had envisioned
yet, his mission was never clear to me.

I was allowed visitations from my father
every Thursday and every other weekend
per the agreement he had signed.
I was unable to discuss with him
the things that were being conducted
but I assure you
it wouldn't have taken a scientist to see
how rapidly I began to change.

Instead, we often played games
talked about mom here and there
reminiscing of her gentleness
before we would each exploit an emotion.
Before long however
I started to feel less and less
and father would call me out on it
when he would catch me zoning out.

"Son, you know you can say stop
at any time if it's too much for you.
Dr. Larson has made that clear."

"If I ask to stop
I'll be showing weakness,"
I retorted.

What I really wanted to say however was
'There is no such thing as saying stop.'
That was just a comfortable lie my father was fed
in order to keep him compliant.

Create Destruction

My father wasn't one to overreact
but he had been known to be reactive to situations
that initiated the fight or flight survival instincts
due to his stint in the early months of the Korean War.

By the time I was three years old
and the government made their deceptive promises
to care for and assist my mother in his absence
my father volunteered to fight overseas
to protect his growing family.
He had only been gone for 14 months
to which he was tortured
stripped of a limb
and a prisoner of war for over four months.

Father was quiet about the war when mother was alive
but he had no one else to confide in after she passed
thus, he shared some of the horrors
he witnessed and lived through
with me.
It wasn't known to either of us at the time
that Dr. Larson monitored our conversations
providing him with crucial information about my family's history
as well as effective and clever ways of torture.

Ryan A. Kovacs

There is a hornet called the 'Vespa Mandarinia'
also known as
the Asian Giant Hornet
that releases a pheromone on its prey
in order to direct more hornets from the colony
to the source it is about to attack.

The sting can be lethal in large doses
sending victims into cardiac arrest or anaphylactic shock
causing a rather slow and painful death.

My father sustained such a sting from a hornet
while imprisoned in Korea
where interrogations
and nonsensical experimental murders were conducted.

Taking a page out of recent history from the Germans
the Korean soldiers found new inhumane testings of torture
to extract information from soldiers
or sometimes
they did it just for fun.

Through trial and error
they were able to find out which soldiers had allergies to bees
and exploited such weakness in the men who were captured.
In so, they would release the giant hornets into a room
where a prisoner would be covered in tree sap
and the moment the hornets were drawn to the food source
they would begin to sting the man
releasing the pheromone into the air to alert the other hornets
where the food was
repeating the lethal injections all over the body until dead.

Create Destruction

"Lieutenant Lauber was one of the last to fall victim,"
Father sighed.
"When our platoon was outflanked and outnumbered
the Koreans led us to a small hut village
where they performed monstrous acts of evil upon us.
Each day was randomized
and if anyone survived the torture
they would just get thrown back in the cell
and recycled for the next day.
The LT got selected four days in a row
and on the fourth day
he met his match with the Asian Hornets."

Father chuckled to himself briefly as he exclaimed
"Lieutenant Lauber was the hardest son-of-a-bitch I ever knew
and easily the greatest leader I have ever come to know.
The guy never made his men do something he wouldn't dare do
and that, I believe, set him apart from any other leader."

He cleared his throat
as he started to choke up.
"That fourth day was the day we were liberated—
when our brothers in arms came to our rescue.
I had already lost my arm by that time
and felt like I would die any day.
That day should have been the day
had LT not taken my place
volunteering to receive the torture for the day instead of myself.

Once the Koreans had been eliminated and fled the area
I ran to the room where he had been tortured
opening the door to a small swarm of giant hornets
that buzzed on past me
until one stung my flailing arm.
I swear to you son
it felt like a hot nail being driven into my forearm
just from the individual sting
so I cannot even begin to fathom
how Lieutenant Lauber must have felt

having dozens all over his body.
When I reached him
his body was about as warm as a bed of coals
all puffed up and swollen
choking on what little air he could breathe
as his airways began to close.
I sat there
holding his hand
and witnessed him choke to death.
The medic affirmed me saying
he had died well before I'd gotten there from shock
and that the body was still spasming
but I knew that was just a lie he told me in order to keep me calm."

Create Destruction

I had a sister.
Or at least the idea of having one.
She was taken before she was born
shortly after Dr. Larson had recruited me
and I was no longer home as often.

Ironically around that same time
is when my mother's health began to decline
after ten years of seemingly getting by
despite the damage both radiation and cancer had done to her.
She and father talked about having more than one child often
but had fears of mother being infertile due to her treatments.

Yet somehow they were able to conceive
and when they shared the news with me
father seemed so sure
while mother had a sense of unease about her.
She did not want anyone to know her discomfort at the time
and wanted desperately to share good news
however, at the six month check up
it was determined that the baby no longer had a heartbeat.

To say my parents were crushed by the news
would be equivalent to them both
sticking their hearts in a vice and slowly turning it
tightening and gripping them until flat and bloodless.
Each of them naturally blamed themselves for the tragedy
despite the begging questions I had—
was I the reason mother was infertile?
was I the reason mother didn't get sick?
Because after mother's miscarriage
her cancer came back

and I was no longer at home.

Ryan A. Kovacs

We lived on a street called Greenway Boulevard
that was anything but what the name had implied.
Arizona was basically brown grass and sand
and that is how I remembered it.
Growing up I had a challenging time pronouncing boulevard
until I saw the abbreviation for it spelled 'blvd'
to which, I would say I lived on Greenway b l v d.

It was a quaint street
feeling more substandard than the outlying suburbs
but regardless, it was home.
Most of my memories there were happy
and revolved solely around the idea
of what all families must endure from time to time—
                                                                pain.

Create Destruction

"I assure you Thomas, that this will indeed be painful.
But it will teach you to control pain—
how to use it on command
allowing others around you to feel as you feel,"
Dr. Larson started.

"Before you is a picture
and I want you to study it deeply
because the word you think of and identify with
will be your pain.
Are you ready?"

I nodded in dismay
uncertain if I was ready to endure what Dr. Larson had promised.
He gave the signal
and behind me a guard came to tighten my straps in the chair
as well as wipe tree sap
along my chest, shoulders, and arms.
Dr. Larson stood up from his chair
placing a photo of our house before me
as he exited the room.

Above me I heard brief static
coming from a speaker in the corner of the room
before the doctor's voice spoke once more
"Thomas, I want you to focus on my voice for a moment…"
he paused.

"Think of your word.
Hold it dear to you because it is what will get you through this.
In a moment we are going to release a swarm of
Asian Giant Hornets.
They can kill you if you are stung enough.
However, I want you to concentrate on each sting you feel
and every time you are stung, I want you to yell your word.

Here we go…

Head."

Ryan A. Kovacs

My eyes locked on the wall ahead of me
and an unusual sensation began to rise within me
as my focus was dialed in on my sense of hearing.
It was as though everything
had been amplified to the umpteenth degree
while I could hear the buzzing and fluttering wings
of dozens of hornets
racing towards my body.

When the first one landed on my shoulder I flinched
anticipating pain upon colliding with me
but moments passed before I suffered my first sting.

It was as father had described
a hot nail being driven into my skin
the first time
to which I screamed my word—
"Boulevard!"

Saying the word aloud was rejuvenating
as I clung to the word and meaning it possessed
before being stung once more—
"Boulevard!"

Soon, each sting that pierced my skin
felt hotter and hotter
like a fire poker being jabbed into my chest
matchsticks searing my nipples
or boiling water being injected into my shoulders—
"Boulevard!!"

I began to scream in terror
heightening my inner senses towards numbness
bellowing my maddening word of pain—
"BOULEVARD!"

The intensity was so grand
that before long I noticed the hornets
attempting to fly away from me

Create Destruction

until I reached out my hand
gripping it as if they were within my palm
piercing the air with my voice once more
while Dr. Larson's voice reverberated over the intercom—

"Boulevard."

Ryan A. Kovacs

Like watching a second hand on a clock
fall one tick at a time
I witnessed each hornet go limp in the air
plummeting to the granite floor
blinking with each smack of their dead bodies.

Unlike the first time I found my word
I did not rise from my chair
yet discovered a new ability within me
as I had begun to emit poisonous amounts of radiation
in every direction.

Create Destruction

Ironically, that same radiation that would bane others
was that same poison that coursed through my veins
never once harming me.

While the pain I had endured could not be undone
my body never absorbed the venom from the hornets
leaving me completely unscathed
with radiation coursing through my veins
attached to each of my blood cells that rejected the toxin.

As medical personnel moved into my aid
Dr. Larson walked gingerly towards me.
Staring down, he spoke satiated
"Your pain is so much more than you can imagine Thomas.
It not only is a power of destruction
but also, a power of creation.
You have within you the potential to be a god…
an actual living god.

I will teach you how to better control your anger and pain
and in so doing
you alone will be the master
of life and death."

Life and death.
Life and death.
I repeated it in my mind like a needle stuck on a record.

Round and round the words tripped within me
like a stumbling drunk making his way home
until he grew sober finding out that his home
was at the bottom of a bottle
where pain was numbed
and thoughts were forgotten words
he never knew he would regret.

What I would have done
to remember then
what I forced myself to forget—

a choice that forever haunted me
was lost inside my pain.

Create Destruction

My father once said
"Where you are in life
is a direct reflection of
the choices you made or failed to make."

So, it is easy to conclude
that after my pain was realized
after its actualization
the point in which I found myself
was further from where I thought I would be.

Ryan A. Kovacs

When father helped engineer the atomic bomb
he and mother were already engaged.
They said they would celebrate their marriage
after the bomb was complete
and that it would represent the goodness the world deserved.

In hindsight, they came to the realization that their dream of virtue
was trumped on the day they were wed
on August 6, 1945.

Their vision
like many others who worked diligently and tirelessly
on the project
believed the bomb to be a scare tactic.
Moreover
they misunderstood its raw power and capabilities.

It was not until they learned of the total number of lives lost
that the illusion of peace
embedded deep in their minds
was nothing more than a matchstick
lighting the world, a fire
that could never be doused.

Create Destruction

My father vowed to never be part of something
he could not finish with his own hands
seeing through the promises of everlasting peace
that only ever begets another war.

So, when the Korean War conflict ensued
he raced to be the first one on the front lines
battling an enemy who would have a fighting chance
when even he must have thought
in war, nobody wins
when we all lose.

Ryan A. Kovacs

It can be argued
that the greatest loss in war
is life.

Yet, I found myself thinking
about the stories my father would tell me of the war
that, however tragic
the loss of life in war is the immediate cost owed.
But eventually every survivor of war
must pay the price
of time.

Like a life that is lost
we don't get our time back
we just suffer with the knowledge
that death is always before us
waiting patiently to claim
the only thing we have left.

So, I had but one question sitting before Dr. Larson
that I asked myself repeatedly over the next few months:

when would it be my time to die?

Ryan A. Kovacs

It had appeared as though
I was invincible
and yet, in a world of capabilities and accomplishments
it only seemed as though
I was invisible.

Create Destruction

In the coming months
I came to learn much pain
through pain itself
as I continued to endure physical torture
that Dr. Larson convinced me was my strength.

The beginning times were but a building block
a way to assemble my obedience
while molding me into an amenable thoughtless being
who had no thought process beyond executing the will of others.

"Do you know why human beings experience pain, Thomas?"
Dr. Larson asked mildly during a routine checkup
with the facility doctor.
The blood pressure cuff was constricting like that of a python
as I slowly felt my fingers begin to tingle
"No, Dr. Larson, I do not."

"Pain is a triggered response by the brain
to alarm an individual that something is wrong
and that whatever is causing that pain
should be stopped or avoided."
He cleared his throat
and looked up at the ceiling
"Humans avoid pain because they do not know how to embrace it.
They fear it because they think it is weakness.
But I ask you
what does an individual become
when he or she overcomes a deep pain
all while enduring and suffering through it?

"They become stronger,"
I replied steadfastly.

"Yes!
You are so right my boy.
It is because that individual
came to terms with that pain
allowing it to be a part of them
ultimately recognizing that it
is only a weakness if they allow it to be."
He brought his attention back to me
"You may not see it right now
but in due time you will come to understand this process
and what you are rapidly becoming.

Create Destruction

This life, these abilities—
they suit you.
They are your armor—
                      your sword and shield—

                                        your reckoning.

You have no equal in this world
and before long
you will be the conductor
of the greatest symphony ever composed
through the screams of our enemies."

Ryan A. Kovacs

"Who are our enemies?"
I asked coyly.

"Everyone who stands in our way.
You may not know it
but the world is still at war.
What we succeeded at in WW2
is what our enemies are vulnerable to.
The world is changing rapidly
but no one is advancing in the same ways we are.

You are our future—
                            our future's history in the making."

Create Destruction

"Thomas, you must understand one important thing
about human nature:
we do not learn unless it is from experience."
Dr. Larson looked tenderly into my eyes
as if instilling innocence in his statement.

"A child does not recognize a stovetop is hot until he touches it.
Despite the warnings and efforts to not touch it
his curiosity will always get the best of him until he himself
learns what that stove is and what it can do.

No different than the society and world we live in
we did not know what the atom bomb was
or what its devastation would be
until we dropped it on millions of people.
We did not know the power it beheld
nor the path it would set us on in seeking you."

"But Dr. Larson
I am not special,"
I admitted lightly.

"You are my boy.
More than you may ever know or understand, frankly."
He nudged a bit closer
almost whispering in my ear
while the doctor finished in the room with his paperwork
"Do you believe in destiny, Thomas?"

"Can't say I know the meaning, Dr. Larson,"
I responded politely.

"Every person on earth is on a path.
No matter a man's beliefs
it is an undeniable fact that
wherever someone is at any given point in life
is a direct reflection of the choices they've made
or failed to make.

While it is perceived that everyone has an amount of control
aiming and guiding them in the direction they seek
the universe beholds coincidences and chances as fractions in time
that can be split into different paths we must travel.
No matter which path we choose
no matter the outside forces that push us towards a decision
no matter the effort we fill each providence with
in the end
we are always exactly where we are supposed to be."

Pondering the question briefly
I hesitated to ask
"Where am I meant to be then, Dr. Larson?"

As if he already knew my question before I had asked
he responded rapidly

"At the end of it all."

Create Destruction

To be stripped of your own free will
your own thoughts and emotions
is as much a task that any man could endure and persevere.
No different than the predator that stalks its prey
with the only mindset to survive
I was at one point full
until one day I was not.

It felt like a light switch
a snap of the fingers
the press of a button
that changed me from a being
into something else entirely.

I was foreign to my own self
as if my soul consciously stepped outside my living body
looked upon me with disgust and distain
rummaging every question surrounding the simplest one—
                                                                    why?

Yet, I was compelled to be a prisoner
shackled amidst my dissolving innocence
that, with each new word that controlled me
would be a nail in the coffin the old me would die in.

Ryan A. Kovacs

I would emerge
something of this world
that would be accepted
but somebody of this world
who was unrecognizable.

Create Destruction

"Thomas, I am going to start counting.
When I reach the number you are comfortable with
say the number before I do."

I nodded in agreement
while I sat in the chair in nothing but my underwear.

"One.
    Two.
        Three.
            Four.
                Five."

I spoke with a rasp in my voice
"Six."

Dr. Larson dipped his head
signaling the guards behind me to restrain me in my chair.
The slightest bit of terror overcame me
until the fear of the unknown began to take over.
Dr. Larson stood from his chair
collecting his papers and pen
walking out of the room
flipping the light switch off.

The giant metal door slowly shut
as the locking mechanism engaged
and I was left alone in the pitch-black room.

A part of me wanted to speak aloud with hopes of some response
but it had become abundantly clear
that it was another test—
another word that would be the third one to control me.

After some time
I began to worry.
Growing hungry and having to go to the bathroom
I cried out
"Hello?
    Dr. Larson?
Anyone?
    Is anyone there?
I don't understand what's going on.
    I'm hungry and I really must pee.
Can someone help?"

I received no reply
not even the faintest glimpse of sympathy
from those who knew what was to come.

Hours must have passed
and with each attempt to free myself from the restraints
my wrists grew more raw
and my bladder filled
until the only immediate relief
was to relieve myself.

Create Destruction

As I sat there
in my own piss and embarrassment
with the now lingering sensation of hunger
I began to feel overwhelmed with confusion.

Questions raced through my mind
like a robber fleeing from police officers in a high-speed chase
weaving in and out of possible answers
but never knowing the reason.

It wasn't until I urinated again
drowning myself in pity and shame
that resulted in such a childish notion
telling myself that it was okay to do it
when I got the idea to attempt what I had been taught.

I knew I could burn through the restraints
as I had done in the past
but needed to trigger myself.

I spoke aloud to myself
"Head.
Boulevard."

But nothing had ignited within.
I tried once more
visualizing my successful attempts in the past.
I took a deep breath
"Head.
Boulevard."

And still
nothing.

Create Destruction

I started to cry.

Weeping like I'd lost a pet
while shivers ran down my spine
with the sudden urge to pee once more.
Trembling from the relieving sensation
I could not bear the thought of my humiliation.

What felt like days
could have been mere hours
as my head hung above my chest
when the lights turned back on.

I opened my eyes slightly
peeking at my now yellow stained underwear
forging an image of indignity
which would smear the image of myself.

Ryan A. Kovacs

A voice crept up behind me through the intercom
"Look what you have done.
You've pissed yourself.
You are a fucking embarrassment.

Let this be a lesson to you, Thomas
that nothing is yours.
You do not choose
you do not want
and you do not have control.
                              I have control.

                                                  Head.

                                                Boulevard."

My eyes widened
and my fists clenched
as the restraints around my wrists bubbled and melted to the floor.
It was the first time however
that a fleeting moment of anger passed through me
when I turned to the speaker
with an attempt to lash out at it
I took one step forward
and heard
                                                        "Six."

Create Destruction

I stopped dead in my footsteps
halted like an obedient dog
whose willingness fought the urge to continue.

A rush of what felt like blood
coursed through my body
like a magnet pulling me from every direction.
I was stuck in place
recognizing the epiphany that slowly became
the only knowledge I had come to know.

I had no control of myself.

Ryan A. Kovacs

The doors opened
and in walked Dr. Larson
empty handed with disgrace on his face.

"Sit,"
he gestured with his hand
watching my internal struggle begin to fade.
Upon sitting
I started to uncontrollably cry once more as he spoke
"Thomas, are you familiar with the eye of the storm?"

I sniffled into the palms of my hands
"Like a hurricane?"
I asked.

"Precisely.
You see, within the raw power of a storm
there is a part of it that is calm.
It is usually the false hope that the storm has subsided
when, in reality, its greatest power and force is to follow.

You are a storm—
the potential to be a perfect storm.
You are within the eye at this moment
when even you think the worst has happened
we have only begun to unlock your abilities.
'Six' is your calm word
and the last word that keeps you grounded to humanity.
The words that accompany
will now be what follows the eye of any storm
the real, raw, uncontainable energy that will be truly unleashed."

Create Destruction

"And now
we start,"
he stated eagerly.

"Start what?"
I whimpered.

"To make the perfect storm."

If I had been drawn up in a lab
on some dusty chalk board
I think it would be safe to say
there would have been many mistakes.
Men of science follow numbers and equations
weighing pros and cons
and the perception that whatever they create
they also have control over.

Perhaps this was what separated Dr. Larson from
scientists and doctors alike.
Men who denied my existence possible
were the same ones that feared my potential
while the men who believed in my abilities
were the same ones who feared the consequences.

When I sat before a panel
of fourteen men who questioned Dr. Larson
about his tests on me
he used the phrases
'Let me be clear'
and
'I assure you'
at the beginning of each statement being made
as if softening the true words that would follow
about what he was trying to accomplish.

"It has been four months, Doctor
and we still do not have a demonstration of the power
you claim to have unlocked,"
a man stated indifferently.

"I assure you that the government's money is not going to waste
if that is what you are implying.
You never gave me an ultimatum to provide a demonstration
now all of a sudden you're demanding to have one?
The results you seek take time,"
Dr. Larson argued.

Create Destruction

"You have six months to provide a demonstration of power
or the U.S. Government will pool its resources elsewhere."

"Let me be clear
the mind is a fragile thing
and to dissect it while keeping it intact
is not a petty homework assignment
that can be turned in the following day.
What I am doing is a breakthrough in science and human law.
I need time or the consequences could be catastrophic,"
Dr. Larson stood poised.

"Six months, Doctor.
This meeting is adjourned."

Ryan A. Kovacs

Dr. Larson scoffed at the men as they emptied their seats
leaving the underground facility
to emerge from beneath the ground where I lied dormant
like some tamed beast
awaiting my day for release
to see the sun once again.

The months in captivity
felt like a form of torture
while breathing nothing but vent smelling oxygen
clean linen and polished boots
unable to feel the vibrant warmth of the sun
but rather the damp emission of fluorescent light
that blurred my vision every time they turned on.

I sighed under my breath from the wish to see the day
just before Dr. Larson grabbed me by my shoulder and muttered
"We will need to double our efforts, Thomas.
No stone unturned and no holding back.

The U.S. government wants a demonstration of power
we will see to it that they get what they desire."

He locked eyes with me
"Tomorrow, we build the storm."

Create Destruction

And so it was
as he foretold
Dr. Larson became the conductor
about to create the greatest symphony

and I was the music.

Ryan A. Kovacs

Sequence II
Collapse

"What we are trying to uncover
is your potential
and at the same exact time
generate a sequence in which it both
channels your abilities
and sustains your life.

We are not trying to kill you
regardless of the methods we use that could kill
any ordinary human being.
All you need to understand is that everything we do
from here on out is
necessary,"
Dr. Larson spoke with conviction.

"If it helps you to break it down
think of this process as three sequences.
The first sequence is for
                              control.
The second sequence is for
                              collapse.
The third sequence is for
                              rebirth."
Dr. Larson looked at me
as if starting the process for the very first time.
His curiosity and thirst for creativity and results
were like him playing poker with his cards facing his opponent.

"This sequence, Thomas
will be very unpleasant.
We will begin to strip away the layers of yourself
that make you, you
because you are not your own anymore—
you are mine."

Create Destruction

The stage was set
the next chapter beginning
and there was nothing I could do to stop it from happening.

"Head...
Boulevard...
Six."

Pulled in from every direction
I was locked and honed in on the voice echoing
throughout the concrete walls that surrounded me
from the intercom system.
Dr. Larson stood behind the thick glass
watching intently at my focus
while two security guards approached me from each side
syringes in hand with clear liquid within.

"Thomas
the men before you are going to inject you with adrenaline
enough to make your heart stop in fact
and all I require from you is a memory.

Tell me about your first childhood memory...
be as detailed as you can,"
Dr. Larson insisted.

Before I could even utter my first word I felt
the pinching of the needle thrust deep into my neck
as the rush that ran over and through me was like that of a bullet.
In the blink of an eye
my heart started to pound heavy against my chest cavity
as if it were a fist pummeling on a door to escape.
I started to speak quickly
"I was with my mother and father.
We were at a local park..."

The next injection went right into the other side of my neck.
My hearing heightened.
My vision sharpened.

It was as if I were becoming tuned in to my own body
that seemed so foreign having never
regulated to it the way I did in that moment.

I closed my eyes to imagine the memory once more
"I was running with my father.
I fell and cut my knee.
My mother ran to my aid, but father told her to stop.
He said I was okay.
He said that I was strong…"

My eyes started to twitch
vibrating within my skull
as my skin began to crawl
and my breathing increased towards panic.

"Where were you?"
Dr. Larson asked.

"A park."

"Where?"
He asked again.

"A park!"
I answered loudly.

There was a brief hesitation in my speaking
then another guard stood before me
and proceeded to drive a needle straight into my chest cavity
while at the same time Dr. Larson spoke clearly through the intercom

"Park."

Create Destruction

My body raged inside with
blood flooding my organs
rushing like white water rapids.
The helpless feeling of paralysis began to settle in
while my vision blackened
ears rang like distant static
and my extremities numbed
until my mind's eye caught a glimpse of the memory I'd shared—
the overbearing truth of loneliness catching hold
of a mother I would never see again
and a father who would teach me no more strength.

So, I breathed.
Deep and slow…
d
 e
  e
   p
    and s l o w
allowing thoughts to catch up to the reality set before me
tuning out the distracting hormone coursing through my body
ignoring its effects and hold.

Trembling among body twinges and muscle spasms
I took hold of myself
a hand reaching its own
knowing the grip to be unwavering
and extended it outwards towards the glass where Dr. Larson stood
displaying my fierce, unrelenting control.

He smiled his devilish grin
and whisked his pen on the notepad before him
with sheer admiration of nothing more than himself.

Ryan A. Kovacs

Trapped briefly in the moment
before unconsciousness fell upon me
I found the first moment of clarity and certainty—
that whatever obstacle was placed before me
whatever test I would be forced to endure
I had a starting point.
From there
who would have known my potential
when I hadn't even known it myself?

Create Destruction

The transient feeling of blacking out
is that of an out-of-body experience.
The existential moment
is so ordinary in relation to being stripped of human emotion.
The numbness and stupefaction are no different
than having the brain rubbed in Novocain
where it fires neurons that spark only from a
triggered response…

and it appeared, that's all I was going to be.

Ryan A. Kovacs

I dare say that the difference between
a child and an adult while trapped in isolation
is simply the lack of hope.

A child will hold steadfast to it.
They will manage to cope without it
finding barriers to wall up their minds
not allowing them to weaken.
Their resilience will stand front and center
and embrace that which is the reality before them.

An adult will give up.
They'll give up because they know something
the child does not—
that hope is wasted on the unknown
and in time
the body and mind will wear down
no different than the stone erodes to water.
They will come to accept their situation
and with that
eventually welcome their fate.

They each will share the same absence
devoid of reason
yet filled with faltering emotions.
What unites them, however, is the glimpse of
that fraction of a second
where the thought empties as quickly as it fills
with the idea
the conceptualization
the perception
of survival.

Then and only then
will each conclude
that hope was just wasted time
while coming to terms with death.

Create Destruction

I solved the problem I'd been fighting
passed out from the abundance of adrenaline
pumping through my body
that none of this would stop
until I did.

And I wanted it to stop
but Dr. Larson wouldn't let me
as he began to peel layers of me away
rebuilding me stronger each time.

With each success came a new failure
thus a new compliance and strengthened obedience.

I knew that the only way to stop
was to die.
It wasn't about when was it my time to die anymore.
It was about learning how.

No sooner did I release my body from a fading thought
and memory
was I ejected from darkness
brought back to light
by yet another shot of adrenaline
punched deep into my heart once more.
I sat up like a vampire from a coffin
my eyes glossed over into strict tunnel vision
ready to jump out of my skin
and into an abyss of vacant space.

Breathing so intensely
as if waking suddenly from a nightmare
I debated the reality I'd been brought back to
with Dr. Larson kneeling before me
holding the empty syringe.

"Catch your breath, Thomas
feel the rush throughout your entire being
and allow it to fill you to the brim
as it molds you into something different, something more,"
Dr. Larson whispered
"We have much work to do."

Create Destruction

Days went by
and as he promised
the very layers he claimed would be peeled
were in fact stripped away and discarded.

Each day brought more adrenaline
repeating and rehearsing the same memory
as if punishing me for the very thing Dr. Larson demanded.

It wasn't until I recalled a conversation
with my father weeks prior
when he told me before departing
our limited and almost non-conversing conversations
"Insanity is doing the same thing over and over, Thomas
and expecting a different result."

Was this the stage of lunacy?

Or was it the part where foolishness would corrupt?

Ryan A. Kovacs

"Again!"
Dr. Larson demanded the guard to inject me.

Pushing the needle into my neck while sitting in the chair
I proceeded to concentrate
not wholly on the hormone rippling through my veins
but on the idea of producing my own inner strength
to keep it at bay.

I steadied my breathing
out then in
out and in
out
        in…

within my mind I started to see a reflection of myself
my pale skin
stained underwear
my dark pointed hair
and fearful eyes.

Approaching my inner self
I reached for my own shoulder
as if to grasp with assurance
instead, upon making contact
that former self began to melt before me
as if witnessing metal pool to the floor like magma.
In turn, I stood before a puddle of my former being
who no longer existed.

Searching my surroundings
I began to lift myself from the metal chair
while the arms began to bow beneath my palms.
The guards in the room with me
started for the door
before Dr. Larson's voice came through the intercom
"That's enough, Thomas."

Create Destruction

With my ears I could hear his words
yet something within me was compelling
almost like an insatiable need to continue
down this new path I'd begun to travel.

"Head...
Boulevard...
Six."

And like snapping fingers
the inner image was gone
evaporated like water from a desert.
With my eyes
the clarity of reality was unrelenting
from what I'd just experienced within
and the smallest piece of me

beckoned to feel more.

Dr. Larson entered the room after a few moments
as chatter outside the room
was filled with panic.

"I assure you
the boy is under my control.
You need not worry about what he will do
as we unlock his latent abilities,"
he spoke softly to the men.

As he approached from behind me
Dr. Larson asked me to walk with him.
Scaling the long white hall
with many mysterious doors
each passerby looked inwardly at me
as if I were an alien.
Some were fear stricken
while others disgusted
instilling my already insecure self-image.

Noticing my diffidence
Dr. Larson raised his voice loud enough
for those within an earshot distance to hear
"Pay no mind to these ineffectual individuals
who have no idea who you are, Thomas."
He spoke louder
"They don't know how important you are."

Grabbing my shoulder
he escorted me into a room
filled with total blackness.
Closing the door behind us
he stood behind me
speaking to me in his ominous tone
"Thomas, there is a darkness in every person.
Each individual finds something there
at some point in their life.
Imagine this as yours
and without closing your eyes

Create Destruction

you must come to accept this as your own.
Embrace it like you would a loved one
speak to it the way you would make demands
become one with it as your body and soul
seek to understand what it calls out to you for
while answering it with unrelenting force and passion."

I gulped.
Swallowing incoherent sounds that
wished to erupt from my throat.

"If you do not seize that darkness, Thomas
this is what you will become."

The lights flashed on
blinding my immediate sight
until I could clearly see
myself before a mirror.
I clenched my fists
bit hard on my teeth
and punched the mirror
watching my reflection shatter.

From the top corner of the mirror
I could faintly see
Dr. Larson's amused smile.

Ryan A. Kovacs

With his smile came the understanding
that it was easy to get lost in the space
which he was guiding me towards
and with the absence of my conscious
I would have nothing to fear
not even myself.

It was my job
my purpose
my duty
to empty everything within me
completely devoid of anything
that made human beings exactly that.

Taking the new knowledge
I centered my focus
and with the wave of my hand
the mirror before me began to ooze from the top
running down like reflective tears
soaking the concrete floor beneath
providing a new backscatter
of what and who I would become.

Create Destruction

It was clear
the driving force of my anger
was none other than I.

The inability to even glance at myself
was the embodiment of self-disgust
that brought on the stable insecurity
of who I was
and with that
the fortitude to change.

"Thomas, in order for you to do what I am asking…
to do what is required
you must not just fill with inner rage
but overflow with it.
It cannot be a bucket or barrel or hole that crests
and empties into some other container to control
what we are trying to break within you.
It must always be brimming
incessant and rigid in form
forever trying to escape
with no way to suppress.

Come.
We will be done for the day
and tomorrow we will be what you need to be."

Ryan A. Kovacs

It is never certain—
if the choices we make in life are the right ones.
"There is beauty in the unknown,"
my mother once told me on her deathbed.
There were aspects of living that I sensed
were only apparent to those who'd accepted their inevitable fates
with death waiting to inscribe the name of the deceased in his book
before departing to the next victim to be called upon.
Mother seemed to linger in her last days
like a stubborn leaf blowing in a snowstorm in winter
when all the other leaves had fallen
yet something kept her holding on.
I know she wanted me to make peace with her demise
while she lived
but it never crossed my mind
how different forever would be for us both.

To her, an eternity was but steps away
a concept she would be a part of—
one I could not begin to comprehend.

"The unknown is a path we all must travel
in both life and death, Thomas.
We must not fear where it may lead us
however, embrace it as our own
declare it as we would our reason for breath.
Then and only then
will we accept our own reality,"
she spoke softly.

I recalled the faded memory
clinching to it like the jaws of a predator on its prey
begging to find reason and justification
in all that had befallen me
and where I was destined to grow
I lay there on my cot
staring at ceiling tiles blackened by obscurity
with empty hopes of waking
with purpose the next morning.

Create Destruction

Purpose is what I ultimately awoke to find that morning
in the form of unceasing thoughts that prodded my mind
of the one thing in life, I truly had no more—
my mother.

I harbored so much pain within the essence of her absence.
The fabrics of decaying memories with age
that forcefully dissolved her from my recollection
because she no longer posed
a physical presence in my life anymore.

Tragically, the mind is cruel in this regard
stripping from us
the love we feel for another who has passed
to add insult only further to injury
by clouding our mind of their memories through erasure.
So too is the purpose of conjoining feelings with memories
that in the event one begins to fade
the other will remind you not to let go.

Yet, Dr. Larson wanted me to let go
to release the grip of pain with hopes of it consuming
rather than restricting.

But how?
How could I endure the agony of letting go of the very thing
that seemingly gave me purpose?

"Do you know what your purpose is, Thomas?"
Dr. Larson asked arbitrarily.
"...No,"
I hesitated with my response.

"It's fine to not know the answer.
Most people in the world don't know it either.
In fact, many spend their entire lives seeking this meaning
only to die without ever knowing.
I for one believe it to be a matter of choice
and not just some happenstance that individuals
stumble upon one day.
Truly, that which we love and seek is in fact purpose
wouldn't you agree?"

I nodded in agreement.

"Then you must understand
what your purpose is by now, Thomas—
to
be
change."

I rebutted
"But you've instilled the vision of creation within me
that, in order to create this new world
the old one must be destroyed."

"You're not wrong, Thomas
but you are missing a key point.
You see, it is my purpose to teach you this lesson
in addition to controlling your powers.
The meaning behind all that however
is as you described, for a new world."

Create Destruction

"What's wrong with this world, Dr. Larson?"
I asked earnestly.

"Mmmmm, Thomas, my boy
THAT is a loaded question…
it bears an answer you may not fully understand
at this moment in time
but I will do my best
to give you an answer satisfactory to your comprehension."
He cleared his throat and sat back in his chair
almost taking a reclined position
like that of a rocking chair
raising his hand to his chin
as if readying for deep thought.

"Human nature is, at its core, predictable.
Within its predictability lies the basic fundamentals
to understand
to believe
and
to choose.
It is an infinite loop that cannot be broken
and yet, within the boundaries of unpredictability
humanity tries to control the trajectories of human nature.
The misconception is that life is not a straight line
that it changes direction due to outside influences
when the reality is, life is a straight line in time
and the end is always the same.
Those outside variables never divert a life
they merely intersect with it
emboldening the already predetermined path.
You see, the connection to all humans is
empathy
conviction and
values—
when one is missing
the rest fall short
and we fail at living.

But you are the embodiment of human nature
which has formed the necessary genomes
giving birth to the only human ever to exist
that will be the true change in human evolution."

Create Destruction

Dr. Larson closed his eyes
envisioning the words that fell from his mouth
"I see you amidst a crowd
able to employ life's final judgement
bringing upon it
both wrath and peace.

When the dust settles
you will be the change
this world deserves."
He opened his eyes wildly
and spoke up
"But it does not come without sacrifice nor consequences
thus, our lesson today, Thomas.
While I know that is a lot to chew on
there is still much work to be done
and the wicked don't sleep
so we better get to it."
He nodded with affirmation
and started towards the exit
"Today you will learn about the world and its lack of
empathy, conviction, and values
and in turn
develop them of your own
so that you may finally have a path to begin to travel."

And with his final word
like a portal opening next to me
I felt the cracking of a boney fist
strike my cheek
sending me sailing to the floor with arms flailing.
Before I had a chance to react
a baton came crashing down onto my back
as I belted out a painful scream.
My body fired pain receptors
with each smashing blow against my body
as I was circled by multiple guards
who tirelessly began to beat me.
I rolled over to my left side
curling into the fetal position
clenching my fists and tightening my muscles
as they absorbed each destructive blow brought down upon it
before I could hear Dr. Larson's calm voice
repeating my name over the intercom
in an attempt to gain my attention.
When I looked on towards the window
he met my eyes with choice words
"Thomas, take a deep breath,"
he started.

With my inhalation
the beating paused and with it
I gathered myself
as my body began to ache and throb.
"A word is required, Thomas.
What is your word?"
Before I could utter a syllable
a synchronized attack bashed my body
then immediately halted.
Wincing through my stollen breath
I could hardly speak but vocalized a word—
"Right."

After the word exited my lips
I once again received uniformed swings onto

Create Destruction

my face, side, arm, and leg.
The strike across my face created a gash next to my eyebrow
where blood began to pool and fall into the corner of my eye.
"Again, Thomas!"
"Right,"
I mustered through choking air
while blows came down again and again.
Bruised and bloodied
bones broken and dislodged
I heard over the intercom once more

"Head...
Boulevard...
Six...
Park...
Right."

The sequence began to stir within me.
With a final blow to my hand gripping my skull
I felt the shattering of bone fragments in my fingers
until I found myself rising from the tile floor
like that of a bird ready to take flight
releasing a scream that reverberated off the walls
sending the guards shooting in each direction of the room
while the tidal wave within me pushed through my skin
exposing weaknesses and turning them to strengths.

Bringing my knees to my chest
I opened my bloodied eye
letting a droplet fall like that of a tear
as I looked on at my broken fingers
that were bereft of feeling.
My body no longer throbbed or ached
yet felt anesthetized and filled with numbness.

Astonished at this self-discovery
I peered up at one of the guards who gathered himself from the floor
"Hit me,"
I demanded.

He looked over at the glass where Dr. Larson stood behind
to which Dr. Larson responded
"Do as the boy requests."

Slowly approaching me
with tamed fear in his eyes
I slowly stood from where I crouched
and met his look with mine.
Winding up as anyone would a baseball bat
he struck the back of my leg
bringing me to my knee.
What should have been increasingly painful
faded as fast as the blow itself against my body.
With might
he began to pummel me
on all my extremities.
While the force may have kept me down physically
my body reacted
as though the human connection to pain had been severed.
Out of breath, the guard stopped and edged backwards
giving me space to reclaim
standing once more hunched over.

Pain free, my body was completely stupefied
and my heart—
steady.

Create Destruction

In the coming weeks
with each iteration of learning to desensitize physical feeling
every beating I suffered
I had no choice but to endure.

So too is life—
the moments that bring us to our knees
the ones that challenge us in order to change us.
There wasn't a lesson to be learned from being devoid of feeling
rather, to live in and through the moments
which pushed me further into the well
of overwhelming power, I could not begin to fathom.

In an all-consuming perspective
shedding what small light remained
in such a growing obscurity within
was with me as it is with us all—
when we stop feeling
       we in turn
              stop living.

Ryan A. Kovacs

I could see it in my father's eyes
the unexpected horror and concern
when I entered our meeting room for our father/son time.
It was the first time he laid eyes on me
while I appeared fragile and broken.
My fingers taped together at each joint
straightened and secured underneath with popsicle sticks—
my face and neck bruised in every shade of cool colors.
Attempting to conceal my arm
bound by a hardened cast
I walked over to sit in the chair across from him
and before I could pull the chair out
he reached over the table
to grab my bad arm with his only good one.

Retracing the lack of reaction to pain in my face
he squeezed my broken fingers
bending them down slightly
until the faintest crack of the wood could be heard.
Peering into my eyes and waiting for a reaction
to which I gave none
he finally spoke
"What are they doing to you, son?"
His voice trembled while his eyes began to well
"What are they doing to you?"
He questioned once more
with aggression rising in his tone.

"I must let go of the feelings
that hold me back from my potential,"
I stated coldly pulling my hand from his grasp taking a seat.

Create Destruction

"That is not an acceptable answer, Thomas.
Look at you!
You have broken bones and bruises along your body.
Your eyes are bloodshot and hair a mess!
You look like you've barely slept or eaten
and been mauled by some vicious animal.
Where is Dr. Larson?
I wish to speak to him about your care…"

I cut him off
"I'm fine, Dad."

"Fine?
You call this fine, Thomas?
Where is your mind?
Under no circumstances is this acceptable or appropriate
to have a child living under these conditions,"
he boldly stated, still standing in front of the table.

The door opened behind me
and the Doctor walked in
clipboard in hand and long white tail jacket blowing
from his brisk walk
"What seems to be the problem here?"
Dr. Larson asked.

"Look at my son!
Do you not see his condition?"
My father spoke up.

"Thomas' condition is well within his capabilities
and he is perfectly fine, I might add,"
Dr. Larson assured.

The tension in the room began to elevate
until my father's voice echoed louder throughout the room
"This is torture and inhumane
and I will not tolerate this treatment towards my son…"

Dr. Larson interjected
"I'm sorry, but you keep referring to Thomas
as your son and his conditions unacceptable
but need I remind you that you surrendered your parental rights
on this document here."
Flipping papers on his clipboard
he showed the document to my father from a distance.
"The document also states
that the means of extracting power from Thomas
shall not be questioned or examined by outside sources
due to the nature of government funding and testing.
Surely you must not want to be removed from these premises
and surrender what little rights remain to see Thomas."

"You won't get away with this mistreatment…"

"Perhaps you would like a demonstration of your son's loyalty
and his commitment to his country?"
Dr. Larson instigated.

"Don't talk to me about loyalty and commitment to my country
when I fought and sacrificed for the freedoms of America!"
My father shouted.

"And how good does it feel to know
that the country you sacrificed for could care less about you
and what you stand for?
Hmmm?
I see the blanket that has been pulled over your eyes
that appears to be star spangled to you
but is drenched in blood to me.
You're not seeing the other side because you choose not to,"
Dr. Larson retorted.

Create Destruction

"You don't get to stand where you are right now
without men like me who fought
to preserve freedoms for this country.
I witnessed men die
and was part of the biggest project in human history
that took millions of lives in an instant.
What do you know about sacrifice, Doctor?"
My father rebutted.

Dr. Larson's voice edged towards anger
"I get to stand here because I know more about sacrifice
than you will ever know.
And while I don't need to justify anything
about my personal life nor my work here at this facility
I will tell you that this can go one of two ways:
You can walk on out of here and go on with your miserable life
holding on to the only relationship you have left
with our agreement for visits intact
or you can be escorted from this facility permanently
to have no contact with your son ever again.
It's your choice."

"Tsk," my father sighed with disappointment.

Walking back over to me, my father leaned down
to whisper in my ear
"Don't be what they tell you, my son."

"Will that be all for today?"
Dr. Larson asked implying leave from my father.

"Yeah.
I will be back next week to see my son again."

"Of course, you will,"
Dr. Larson said gently.

Ryan A. Kovacs

And as a final act of insult
I saw from the corner of my eye
Dr. Larson extend his right arm in exchange for a handshake
to which my father could not meet
until he walked off.

Create Destruction

Dr. Larson approached me
laying his hand upon my shoulder
lightly grasping my upper trap
he spoke assuredly
"Do you see it now, Thomas?
The lack of empathy
that leads to deficient conviction
ultimately surrendering one's values…
your own father is part of the world that begs to be cleansed."

I pushed his hand away exiting from my chair.
"You don't know my father,"
I stated with humility.

"I know him enough to say that he sees this world for what it is
no different than you and me
which is why he gave you up."

I stopped in my tracks.
Rehearsing his words in my mind over and over…
'He gave you up'
'He gave you up…'

Without a thought I began to turn around
slowly facing him like light on a sundial
"He did not give me up.
I told him I wanted to be here."

"And he had every opportunity to say no
but he didn't.
He made his choice to discard you, Thomas.
Every man has a choice."

"What about my choice?"
I edged.

Dr. Larson smiled his evilest of grins
                                      "Let me demonstrate your *choice*."

"Head…"

"No.
Please,"
I began to beg.

"Boulevard…"

"Dr. Larson, please."

"Six…"

The channel locks inside my brain began to clamp down
immobilizing my ability to move or think.

"Park…"

Stiff as a board
with my eyes glazing
it was as if I were outside myself
watching my body slowly comply.

"Right…"

There I stood
vacant and absent of thought
while Dr. Larson approached me
"This is what you chose, Thomas.
It's what you choose every day
and because of this choice
your voice will echo throughout all time."

Create Destruction

Time.

A construct built by those who fear the past
are unable to see the future
and thus waste the gift that is the present.

In all the tenses of the conceptualization
it did not appear to me
that I had a place among any of time's keepings
yet I was promised through the termination of thought
if I could rid my past
live through my present
and look towards my future
I would live between the moments of
minutes and seconds
that would establish my place among time.
When, where and how would no longer require an answer
because my presence would be known.

While we may think we know time
it is the fallacy we've chosen to believe
because time is unknown and infinite.

"How long will you continue to take this, Thomas?"
my father asked me the following week
from when he last stormed out.
His attitude appeared less concerning, rather, more annoyed.
"I mean, what is it the mad doctor believes will come
from torturing and hurting a twelve-year-old child?"

"He believes that with pain and suffering
comes empathy and conviction,"
I cited.

"What do you believe?"
his question seemed warm all of a sudden
almost like he'd gestured an invisible hand upon my shoulder
assuring me, whatever answer I spoke was acceptable.

With slight hesitation as if giving thought, I answered
"I believe he is trying to destroy
all the pieces that make me human."

"How's that even possible?"

"You already know how it's possible, Dad.
You saw it when I was growing up.
You saw it the day you signed me over to Dr. Larson.
You saw it last week when you grabbed my hand."
I paused for a moment to gather my building emotions.
"...I'm, beginning to not feel anything anymore.
I wouldn't go as far as saying I am immune...
but I'm numb.
My efforts to hold back have brought me more pain
than my efforts of letting go and accepting the truth."

"What truth, Thomas?"
My father beckoned.

"The truth that I am a weapon.
I don't get to be anything other than that
because this is my fate...my destiny."

Create Destruction

"Are those your words or the mad doctor's?
He asked irately.

"Nothing is mine anymore.
Because, at the end of the day
nothing matters—
not you, not me, not Dr. Larson, not the people in this world…"
I hid my head towards my shoulder
looking into a distance that was not there
escaping into a childhood memory
that faded with each passing day
of a happy child and two loving parents.
"Nothing matters because we have lost the meaning of life.
Until we understand that once again
we are only ever moving backwards in time."

"Son, hear me now and believe me later—
the meaning of life is not around us…
it comes from within us."

'From within.'
A foreign, yet benign thought to ponder
while I lay on the concrete floor of a room
where beatings crushed me from above
as five men wailed my broken body with
fists, feet, and weapons alike.

My arm confined in a white cast stained with blood splatter
butterfly stitches along my brow, cheek, and forehead.
Bloodied spit caked between my teeth
alongside bruises that ranged from all colors of the rainbow
up and down the length of my frame.

All I could feel was the thumps on my body
like lifting and dropping a bag of sand repeatedly.
It was futile to resist
but I wondered, to what end?
Where was this leading?
What would this accomplish?
The wear down was rapid
with my body unable to recover quicker than it was broken down.
I'd proven I could endure
yet it had not satiated Dr. Larson's thirst for torment.

Create Destruction

Over the loudspeaker
I honed in on the doctor's voice
while the guards halted their attack.
"That's enough.
Bring the boy to the infirmary."

While my feet were gliding across the floor
as my limp body was being dragged
I had the inability to feel pain
and the ineptitude to move joints or body parts
that had been broken or severed.
Much like my extremities
the blood that pooled into swollen muscle and tissue
disguised my overall appearance
while other guards and personnel looked on at me with distain.
Almost thrown onto the bed
a nurse came close to me and before she could hook up a picc line
Dr. Larson came in behind her stating
"That won't be necessary
you may leave us."

She nodded and made her exit slowly shutting the door.

My breathing was labored
like I had run a marathon
with my body frantically assessing internal injuries
and ways to heal that it was incapable of doing.

Dr. Larson sat in the nearby chair and spoke
just above a whisper
"Thomas, I want you to close your eyes for a moment
and take a deep breath.
Stay inside this moment for as long as you can.
Listen to my voice and follow it
wherever it may lead you."
I did as he instructed to the best of my ability
while he began once more.
"With your prowess to not feel pain
I want you to envision it.
Imagine if you will
using all your senses with your mind's eye
the internal pain that resides and wishes to escape.
Take hold of those images that flash and flutter…
Embrace them with each breath now."

Create Destruction

With my eyes closed I brought to life
visions of burning fire
the crackling of flames dancing atop of logs—
I could almost smell the dankness of ash
while warmth extended to every crevice of my body.
"What do you see, Thomas?"

"I see fire."

"Ah, yes.
Picture it growing.
Horizontally and vertically.
Stretching upwards and outwards
as it swallows all it touches."

I watched the fire take amebic form
flowing without rhythm
all-consuming and radiating.

"Now imagine it halting.
It has nowhere else to go
and has scorched everything it touched.
The land is blackened and only embers remain.
Smoke rises like fog
revealing the desolate land."

His voice soothed me
paving a pathway for my mind to follow
"What grows in the wake of this destruction?"
He asked solemnly.

Searching around the visualization I'd conjured
alone, I stood atop of smoldering cinders
peering off into the distance to find an unscathed plant.
Approaching it
I gazed with amazement at its resilience while it began
to bloom the closer I moved.
I reached down to pluck it from its place among the gray
as the pedals beamed with orange like the sun.

Comfort passed over me
reminiscing of my mother with Dr. Larson asking
"What grows?"

With the smallest smile I blithely answered
"A flower."

The lily was my mother's favorite
and in both reflection and conception it was the
beginning and end
of
reality and fiction.

> *"Head...*
> *Boulevard...*
> *Six...*
> *Park...*
> *Right...*
> *Flower."*

My eyes popped open
like releasing a cork on a bottle of wine
while vigor rushed through my body
tightening muscles
widening pupils
electrifying nerves
pulsating blood
and enhancing movement.
The tidal wave that engulfed me
spread like a virus
using me like a host who'd serve with unwavering loyalty.

Soon thereafter, my breathing calmed
and throbbing nulled
before the fleeting temporal dimension I'd created within
disappeared with an exhale
giving birth to infinite healing.

Create Destruction

Rising from the bed
I dangled my legs off the edge
able to freely move my extremities
until I hopped off and found the closest mirror.
Examining my body
that had erased all bruising
closed all wounds
and mended broken bones
I stared at the cast on my arm
and proceeded to smash it against the wall
cracking it as if concrete.
I began to tear into it
ripping it from my skin like that of a rabid animal
until it was freed.
Grasping it with my other hand
I made a fist and concluded for the first time ever
that I was not of this world.

I was something
                            more.

Ryan A. Kovacs

Sequence III
Rebirth

Ryan A. Kovacs

Everyone has his own breaking point.
Physically, emotionally, psychologically.
We as humans have found ways to cope
to navigate challenges in hopes of growth.
But what is growth if fate is preordained?
What is choice if destiny is written?
What is purpose if cause and effect are just occurrences?

In a world that asks more questions
than it demands answers
the human race has succumbed
to the one thing it has tried to capture—
                                  control.
In and of itself
the illusion of control is in fact controlling
which always begs the real question—
who is the one in control?

There must be one—
one that directs
one that influences
one that suggests
one that pushes
one that ultimately chooses.

But therein lies the rub—
                       choice.

It is our free will to choose.
On the contrary
our willingness to choose what or who to control.

I walked into my concrete room
the bed replaced with a cot
the toilet replaced with a bucket
the white lights replaced with red ones.
The door shut behind me
the locking mechanism engaged
and it became abundantly clear to me
the next stage of my evolution was here.

Create Destruction

Sitting on my cot
listening to the fabric stretch over the metal beams
the twisting rubber sound echoed in what now felt like a chamber.
This was the kind of place
they sent people to go mad.

And I must have known it to be so
when I asked myself the greatest question of my life
did I choose to relinquish control
or
did I control the choice altogether?

Ryan A. Kovacs

In this new solitary confinement
I found the greatest torture of all was indeed
my mind.

The distances it would travel to recover a memory
the lengths it'd stretch to feel some kind of emotion
the inconceivable thoughts of fantasy that slowly became reality.
I thought to myself **pacing in my six-by-six square**
feeling like some **caged animal**
having committed no crime.
What did I do to deserve this?

Food being dropped off and thrown on the floor
corn and peas scattering across the tile
skipping like stones along the top of a lake
dried out meats tasting like that of chalk
drying my mouth no different than the desert.
I started to tally my meals to keep track of time
scraping my knuckle until it'd bleed
marking the concrete before my body began to heal.
Overfilling my toilet bucket
and unable to shower
the stench in the room from feces and body odor
cauterized my senses
while my new normal set in rapidly.

The red lights that never dulled or turned off
gradually became my only way of sight
like a permanent lens embossed along my cornea.

My animal instincts began to overcome
when food was delivered I'd run to it and scarf it down
then relieving myself without any care.
Sleeping on the cot that absorbed my stench and sweat
grew darker and darker with every sleep
while the production of thought was produced less and less.

Create Destruction

Suddenly my sight was blinded
when the metallic door opened wide
exposing a shadowy figure.
Unable to see his face with my arm covering my eyes
his unmistakable voice guided me
"Thomas, I wish to leave you with a thought
one you may have already asked yourself by now.
The reason you find yourself in this place
is not for my pleasure
but for your gain.
There are but three more words
before your transmogrification is complete
and the storm must rage on.
It's time to be less
so you may be more."
And with the end of Dr. Larson's sentence
the door shut once again
locking me inside
and within my own head.

I had not known the duration of my confinement
but at the rate at which my mind battled hope
it felt like a lifetime.
When I was released
rather than allow me to shower or eat
my malnourished and repugnant body
was escorted before Dr. Larson
who sat across from me unfazed at my appearance.
"I know what I did to you was cruel—inhumane.
I know that you have been treated like an animal.
This was in preparation of this moment however
so that you could emerge from such tribulation.
You know what is required
but before I hear your answer
I want you to reflect for a moment on the past six weeks."

Six…weeks…
A month and a half of being captive
held against my will without knowing a reason—
for which there didn't seem one was even justifiable.
Weeks of pure torture
my mind racing with no finish line to cross.
My body deprived and starved
withering to necessity to live.
Encompassed by my own foul like some pig in a pen
practically fed scraps with no care if I lived or died.
I started to rise
something fueling me
pumping my heart to beat faster and faster.
An inner calm no longer ceasing
began to catch fire from within
as the tipping point reached its unwillingness to return.
"Worn,"
I spoke with my teeth clenched.

"I did not ask you to speak, Thomas
now sit back down."

Create Destruction

"Worn,"
I stated louder
with anger boiling in my voice.

"Sit down!"
Dr. Larson exclaimed.
With narrow eyes I squinted into his
and with an act of defiance
I stood erect, ready to stand my ground.
Dr. Larson called for guards to approach me
with the scuttling of leather boots
and jangling keys
the room began to flood with people as Dr. Larson took his leave.
Retreating to his glass room
he calmly repeated the words I tried to resist

"Head...
Boulevard...
Six..."

With the sequence beginning
the men began to approach me.
Steadying my stance and weakened state
I clenched my fists and readied my reactions

"Park...
Right...
Flower..."

Like a lightbulb
I began to glow
emanating an inhuman hue
while emotions consumed no different
than the beating that ensued.
Cracking, twisting, breaking, tearing—
all the sounds were as deafening as a flash grenade
until something inside me reverberated
an echo from the depths of my soul.
A ringing that pierced all within earshot
spewing from my mouth—
screaming until the only sound was static.

Ryan A. Kovacs

With the gathering of air around me
I ripped from it
the molecules that gave life
until all that remained was poisonous gas
that each guard choked and sucked on.

"Worn..."

Create Destruction

I halted
releasing my grip on the air
as my vision began to clear
seeing what I'd begun to do to over a dozen guards.
Lost in that moment of demonstration
it became apparent how crucial those weeks in captivity were
in having no regard for human life
nor my wellbeing
but to actively act and engage upon instinct.
With my rage still bubbling
I began to understand what Dr. Larson meant when he said
'I must not just fill
but overflow with it.'

At the time, I was undoubtedly unfazed
by my father's shattered image of me
when he approached after not seeing me for almost two months.
His confusion collided with dread
while he touched me lightly on my shoulders and arms
whisking his fingers through my hair in disbelief
until tears welled and streamed down his face
"What has he done to you?"
He asked rhetorically.

I had no answer that would provide comfort.
The truth was ugly and would not go down well.
I just looked off into the distance
lost in both reality and fantasy
as his words became
silent lips moving without purpose.

"Dad, I need you to leave."

"I'm sorry, what?"
He questioned sternly.

"There is nothing left for you here.
I am not who you thought I would be…
not the son…"

"Stop.
I beg you.
Do not say what you're going to say,"
He interrupted.
Gathering himself
he rehearsed what I imagine
he hoped he'd never have to say
"Thomas, sit for a moment.
Just listen to what I have to say
and then I'll do as you request."
I sat down and looked deep into his watering eyes.

Create Destruction

"Your mother and I were not prepared to have you when we did.
Heh, so to it seemed, with every obstacle we faced together
preparedness wasn't quite our strong suit.
We managed though, even when we thought we could predict
what would happen next, and we were blindsided
we always found a way to endure,"
He reminisced.

"That's what our family does, Thomas—
we endure.
Sometimes for strength
sometimes for progression...
sometimes because we just fucking have to..."
He started to choke up.

"When we lost your sister
we were so prepared to have another child...
so ready to grow as a family.
We were not prepared to lose her though—
no parent ever is.
In turn, we held on tighter to you
because our fear of losing another child
far outweighed our love it seemed.
Before your mother passed
she made me promise to never hold you back
to let you make your own decisions and choices
no matter what or how I felt about them
because she knew my fear of letting go
was stronger than my will to hold on."

He took a few deep breaths and continued
"I say all of this because there's going to come a point in your life
sooner rather than later
when you're going to be forced to make a choice
even if you don't think you have any control of that anymore.
When you choose
I hope you will understand my position
and the lesson I had to learn, the hard way, while letting go.
The day you said you wanted to do this

to be where you are
to have what you have
was the day I separated myself from my fear.
You taught me that sometimes holding on
hurts more than letting go."

Create Destruction

I perked up for a moment
contemplating the words he spoke
that resonated in the most profound way.
It made more sense than anything I'd ever known at the time
and felt like the missing link
that would tie my story together.
If my father could let go of his tragic past
consumed with nothing but loss
surely I could do the same.

To do so however, I had to sever my past
the same way his arm was—
the same way his love was—
not gradual
but at once.

"In order for me to do as you have, Dad
you know what I must ask.
Do you wish to hear it once more?"
I contested.

"No, my son.
I know what must be done.
I will leave you with two final reminders
as you finish this journey:
first being, that I love you and am proud of you.
You are my son, my blood, my everything
and there isn't anything that would ever change that.
Lastly, you must remember
you are not what they tell you, you are.
You are what you believe you are,"
he finished.

Ryan A. Kovacs

In an instant
I recalled every leave my father took from home
notoriously speaking Italian to my mother
as he spoke his last word to me,
"Ciao."

And with it
he moved from his chair
exiting without hesitation
while the reality of disbelief settled in
that I would never see my father again.

Create Destruction

Sitting back at a 45-degree angle
staring into bright incandescent lights that appeared like the sun
I recalled the interaction
like a film on repeat.
The internal struggle was a fierce battle that seemed
no matter the victor
loss was inevitable.
Looking at my bound wrists and feet
I couldn't help but realize the irony
of being trapped in my mind.
Yet, that is what Dr. Larson promised to release.
"Thomas, the procedure I am about to conduct
is for your benefit
and will in turn
loosen or break the chains that bind you.
You are haunted and hindered by your past
and despite your progress
you're still missing a piece that makes you, not you.
We must rid your memory
allow the flood to break through the dam
and wash away the lapses of your past that anchor you."

He picked up a small hammer and what appeared to be an ice pick
edging towards me as if an archeologist
ready to uncover fossils of the unknown.

"A word is required that will represent your past.
It will be the final word of your design
before we execute destruction.
The word must be powerful and hold more meaning than any other
for it is your doorway
your unlocking potential
and full understanding
                                      of what your mission and purpose is."

Ryan A. Kovacs

> *"Head...*
> *Boulevard...*
> *Six...*
> *Park...*
> *Right...*
> *Flower...*
> *Worn..."*

Dr. Larson put the metal pointed tip
just centimeters in front of my eye.
Gripping the chair
I accepted my coming fate
and the change that befell upon me.
With the tapping and clinking of metal
driven up into my skull
I screamed my word to release myself from
my past
my humanity
my life...
"Ciao!"

Dr. Larson did nothing to conceal his smile
because he knew all too well
what was going to happen next.

Create Destruction

Propped up in the chair
I felt two pairs of hands at my back
while the other pair grabbed each of my wrists
and yanked me forward until I sat hunched and limp.
I was devoid of personality
absent of any emotion—
a shell of desolation.
The doctor looked on at me
filled with jubilation at his accomplishment.
"He's ready,"
he exclaimed to the guards
"Bring him to the test chamber immediately."

Ryan A. Kovacs

I walked lamely to where the guards escorted me
handing me off to a set of scientists
dressed in heavy lead vests that drooped past their knees
while they guided me into a new room I'd never seen before.
It was dark and hollow
and my breathing seemed to echo
in what felt like a cavern.
The chilled temperature was weightless
cooling my rigid body
as lights began to emit one by one
revealing a giant chamber.
The intercom spoke to me like a voice in my head.

"Thomas, you are standing in the largest underground
nuclear testing site in the world.
Two hundred yards of concrete and metal
meant to harness and shield the world in secrecy
of man's greatest achievement—
the atomic bomb.
Many failed and successful tests have been conducted here
and more importantly
the next stage of nuclear evolution begins with you now.
The room is laced with radiation particles
penetrating your body at an incredible rate.
The average human could not stand where you are
for the duration you have thus far
without dying
already proving your capabilities.
What we will do now
is pump the room full of radiation
to have your body fill with it.
By absorbing its qualities and given the final word
you will act the same as every bomb tested in this facility
and unleash your ultimate power.

This will destroy you
and in turn
you will be created
                              into something more."

Create Destruction

The sequence began.

"*Head…*"

The bolt thrown and locked in my mind.

"*Boulevard…*"

The rise of emotion and fall of regret.

"*Six…*"

Images blurred and forgotten swiftly.

"*Park…*"

Pain rising and filling within the expanse of my mind.

"*Right…*"

Brimming with anticipation and accepted reality.

"*Flower…*"

Stepping out into the unknown of my own possibility.

"*Worn…*"

"*Ciao…*"

"Death is not defeat, Thomas.
It is rebirth…"

And, as if standing on the edge of a cliff
clinging to it with just my curled toes
I peered into the abyss
feeling nothing but rage and desire.
Like the eruption of a volcano
shooting tendrils of magma into the air
I too, felt like heat incarnate.
My body began to fill
with invisible radiation waves
expanding vessels and decaying atoms
placing a cause within me
for which humanity could not fathom
while images of total annihilation swarmed my mind.

Despite all that I had endured
through rigorous torture
and thought termination
not one of those instances
nor all of them combined
prepared me for death.

Ryan A. Kovacs

So, I let my body
overfill—
overflow—
overcome—
over and
over and
over again
until I heard the trigger

"Destroy!"

Create Destruction

"Congratulations my boy,"
the whisper came from beside me
as I lied in bed atop cool cotton sheets.
"You have been reborn through pain
and are now as we had intended from the start.
You will be undeniable change
unwavering towards our enemies who wish to thwart
or threaten us with war."

I breathed shallow and asked
"Why me?"

Snapping his head at me
"Why not you?
Don't you see where you are—
what you've become?
You are the epitome
of life and death
culminated in a single being
that no longer requires answers to a past
when the questions of the future are yours to reply.
You are proof
without a shadow of a doubt
what is possible in this world.
You have purpose—
you have meaning—
you have everything."

But I didn't.
I had nothing anymore.
And perhaps that's what made me so dangerous
to the world
                and to myself...

"We have a big week ahead of us.
The government wants a display of your powers
and we must give them a show.
There are a lot of skeptics and non-believers
that need convincing for us to conduct live tests.
Once we have persuaded the right people
we can move forward with the mission and a few more tests."
Dr. Larson paused for a moment.

"I am proud of you, Thomas.
You are a true wonder.
This world does not deserve you—
but they will be grateful."

Create Destruction

It was all very surreal
living in every moment after my death.
To try and make sense of it all felt daunting
because there simply was no reason to explain my existence.
Regardless of what I underwent
logic and belief seldom meet face to face and agree.
Yet, both seemed to have no issues with me
and thus, I continued
moving in the only direction in which I was pointed.

I was a slave to my mind.
A puzzle incomplete missing a piece.
A door unopened with a missing key.
A wanderer lost with no apparent direction.

It never occurred to me
until after my demonstration for the government officials
that this would be my recurring fate—
to live and die
to die and live
on repeat forever
unless I could find a way to stop it.

Ryan A. Kovacs

Epilogue I
Redemption

I was ready.
Ready to be the weapon I had been molded in to
so that I could be the bringer of death and demise.

One final testing of control was all that stood before me
as Dr. Lawson's voice lingered in my mind
when he breathed to me, my refinement
"You are the definition of the great creation of man.
Not even God could create what you are
because you, Thomas, are true perfection."

It had only been days since I'd demonstrated my abilities
for the United States government officials
and Dr. Larson wasted no time
as he continued to test my limits.

Stepping through the blast doors
into the chamber that started to feel like home
there was a loud crash in the control room
as static muffled like trash over the intercom
until a familiar voice reverberated through.

"Thomas!
It's your father.
I don't have much time, so you need to listen
carefully to what I say.
You are not a killer!
I know you have been trained to do the unthinkable
conducting an act that you've been told will have no effect on you.
But I know that deep down inside
that is not who you are.
You are a human being
regardless of the abilities you've undertaken…
at the true core of your self
you
are
human."

Booming pounds could be heard in the background of his words
while muffled voices urged demands.

I ran towards the demonstration window
watching my father's words match his trembling lips,
"Thomas
they are going to send you into a city
to kill millions of innocent lives.
Dr. Larson has brainwashed you
thinking that the world needs cleansing
and that you're the holy water that can purify existence.
Don't give in to him.
Don't give in to this world that wants to damn you
to be the only executioner."

Thunderous smacks on the door signaled a breach
as father's words became more frantic.

"Son, listen to me.
They are going to kill me because I know
what they want to use you for.
Don't be what they want you to be.
You still have a choice.

You always have a choice.
You've had the choice all along."

Upon his final word
I surveyed the thick glass window
grasping for a handle to open a door that was absent.
Banging on the metal
pleading with the men I witnessed encroach on my father
I watched the guards kick him to the ground
until Dr. Larson approached from behind them
waving a revolver at his side
ready to aim
as he fired one shot
into my father's skull.

The tranquility of the gunshot
was like watching a silent movie—
snippets of time
captured in frames
caught by repetitive blinking
with actions that beckoned sound
yet coveted quietness as if stuck
in a vacuum of space.

The image was final
closing abruptly with a thud on the floor
signaling the end…

Dr. Larson looked up at me
seeing my face in the window
as he began to talk to me as if nothing had happened
through the microphone my father had been holding.

"Thomas, everything is fine.
Go back to the chamber and finish the test."

"NO!"
I stated angrily.

He whispered to a guard
who disappeared from my view
hearing tapes rustle over the intercom.

"Thomas, Thomas, Thomas, my boy.
Your father was crazy
feeding you a bunch of lies.
He was sick
and a part of the world that is no different
which needs you to purge it.

Now that he's gone
you have nothing left to hold you back.

You can finally let go and
be who you were meant to be."

My vision blurred
staring into the puddle of blood under my father's slain body
that seemed to repel around Dr. Larson's shoe.

I felt something start to rise within me
and before it could erupt
I heard the words...

"Head...

Boulevard...

Six...

Park...

Right...

Flower...

Worn...

Ciao..."

I was locked in
as if some invisible force field bound me
fastened to my position
while my mind attempted to process the moments prior.
Standing there for a brief moment
Dr. Larson moved closer to the window
making direct eye contact with me
blocking the murderous scene behind him
"Now that you are compliant
I order you to move to the back of the chamber
to conduct your final test."

I heard his words
yet something I had not felt before
steadied my hands firm against the glass
as heat began to flow from my fingertips and through my palms.
They twitched violently back and forth
with my muscles tightening through each tendon and fiber
beginning to glow and radiate a pale yellow hue.

Dr. Larson's eyes widened
with apparent fear
taking small steps backwards
unveiling to me once more
my father's assassinated body.

Nodding to the guard
Dr. Larson yelled
"Code Red!"

"But sir,
there is the final key word!"
The guard shouted back.

"No!
He is not in the containment chamber
he can destr…"
he stopped himself suddenly before uttering the final trigger word.
"Get more guards down here now!"
Dr. Larson demanded.

The next wave of guards were minutes behind
and in some strange way
I welcomed the idea of uncertainty that was before me.

Pushing my hands deeper into the window
the glass began to overheat
turning a bright orangish-yellow
until chunks melted
falling like ooze to the floor
opening a doorway which I had created
as if stepping through a portal.

The first guard came at me as I exited the molten walls
with the butt stock aimed for my temple
as he attempted to plunge it earnestly into my head.
To his surprise however, I caught his wrist with my glowing hand
gripping it like a vice
listening to his scream erupt like a volcano
while his skin began to soften
running down his arm like sap from a tree.

Within seconds I poured my anger into my blood
letting it boil until it caught fire to the closest thing to me.

Setting the guard ablaze
I watched him fall to the floor like a smoldering campfire
while his gear and weapon fell into the pile of ashy slosh.

With my senses dialed in
I could hear the racking of a round in the rifle chamber
as if it were me who was doing it from around the corner.

The second guard stood before me raising his weapon
with intent to kill.

Pulling hard on the trigger
the bullet shot towards me
and with a static scream I pushed from me a wave-like barrier
that upon making contact with the bullet
it disintegrated like blowing dust.

Taking my hands
I thrusted them forward
forcefully pushing the man against the wall behind him
with a surge of radiant energy.
Stuck against the wall
as if being crucified
I focused all my energy into his body
witnessing his figure expand to twice its own size
before exploding all over the room
drenching the white walls in total red.

Down the hall I heard Dr. Larson yelling
over the blaring siren
"Shoot to kill!"

Running footsteps of steel-toed boots
approached me rapidly
until I stepped into the hallway
catching the half dozen men by surprise
lurking towards them with pure distain.

Before they could ready their weapons
I shot heat at the floor
liquefying the metal in their boots to their toes
as each man dropped to their hands and knees
releasing their weapons while reaching to their feet
in agonizing pain.
With the stench of burning flesh and leather
I shot billows of steam from my body in each direction
turning their polished uniforms into scorching jelly
that stuck to their pores and hairs like hot tar.
Their screams were insatiable
until I heard each of them stop
giving out their final breaths upon me walking by.

Just past them
I gazed at Dr. Larson
whose smirk was as available as the words he attempted to speak
before I sent a ripple of poisonous gas
swirling around him
as he choked stumbling against
the nearest door handle he could cling to.

Falling into the room he'd now opened
men wearing gas masks emerged
staring at me as if I were some demonic creature
risen from the deepest depths of hell
until I shot another wave of heat radiation at their heads
synching their masks to their skin permanently.
Muffled terrors broke from the canister seals
while they dropped to their knees frantically trying to pry
the liquified rubber from their faces.
I made eye contact with them both
before delivering their final fear of death
through endless radiation from each of my palms.

When I blinked it was as if being born
and seeing for the first time
while I shot a glance at Dr. Larson.
Relentlessly, I walked towards him
having not thought about everything I'd just done
until I reached his gagging body
extending my hand to his.

"Is this what you want?"
I asked assertively.

Removing the grip of poisonous air from around him
I gave him the opportunity to speak to me.
Catching his breath through retching coughs
he stared at me in true admiration.

"Yes, Thomas.
This is who you are.
Look what you have done!
It is truly remarkable and unfathomable.
You have total control of your abilities now
because you have nothing holding you back."

We all have a voice inside ourselves
the one that speaks louder than any other ever could.
I learned how to tune that voice out
how to mute it even amidst silence.
But there was nothing left to say
and nothing left to hear
so I just let that voice scream for the first time
the most incoherent cry
my inner self had ever heard.

"Look at how perfect you truly are my boy.
You have the power…"

I interrupted Dr. Larson reaching out to touch his face
"I have the power to choose.
That is and will always be my greatest power.
And I choose to not need you anymore."

I cupped his cheeks between my hands
pushing against them like walls slowly closing in.
His eyes burst open with unyielding terror
trying to plead with me one last time
"Thomas, you can't do this.
I order you to stop!"

I squeezed harder
spilling rays of radiation into his face
watching years befall upon him
as his hair began to curl and fall from his dome
with wrinkles on his head rolling like desert dunes
and skin sagging around his jawbone
he gurgled through coagulated saliva in the back of his throat
"But I… am your… creator…"

Peering cavernously into his soul that was about to escape him
I whispered
"And I, am your destroyer."

Dropping his carcass to the tile floor
the sirens wailed with an echoing pitch
sending fragments of sound around me.
I walked steadily back towards where I had come from
opening the door to where my slain father lay
and approached his still warm body.
Staring at his bereft face
I knelt beside him feeling the cool rush of sadness
dive into my coursing blood
like rapids on a river
recalling the irony of the intense moment.

I had not felt sadness in what felt like a lifetime
and despite how foreign it was
the welcoming of it was no different
than a loving embrace of a forgotten friend.
I stayed with it for a brief time before the interruption
of guns clacking
and footsteps hastening down the halls
converged on my location
suggesting that I to, would suffer the same fate as my parents.

A fate surrounded by uncertainty
that begged understanding
was not how my story would end.
It was as if I were cursed
having lost all the people most important to me
with underlying consequences
which pointed back at me.
I thought briefly about a joyful time
one with smiles and life
and no sooner did I recall it
did it disappear with the blatant reality
that it did not exist.

And neither should I.

I decided in that second
to honor them both with the last choice I had:
not to conform
nor be a slave to the system that created me
yet be courageous within the undeniable truth
of my meaningful existence.

I stood before my father's body
as if shielding him from the image
of a dozen men raising their rifles on me
with fingers already pressed against the triggers.
I raised my hands outward as if they were wings
readying my form to fly one final time
thinking to myself
"I am ready to die."

And with a sigh of profound relief
I whispered to myself

"Destroy…"

About The Author

Ryan is the author of The N.M.E., his first novel in verse, and is known for a unique writing style with philosophical underpinnings. He resides in Churchville, New York where he has simplified his life by being more focused on his children. He is an avid cook and extends his creativity to each and every meal. More often than not, he can be found telling an elaborate story with a cold brew in hand.

Made in the USA
Middletown, DE
23 April 2024